Some
Sexual
Success
Stories

Plus Other Stories
in Which God Might
Choose to Appear

Some
Sexual
Success
Stories

Plus Other Stories
in Which God Might
Choose to Appear

DIANE WILLIAMS

Grove Weidenfeld

New York

Published by Grove Weidenfeld
A division of Grove Press, Inc.
841 Broadway
New York, NY 10003–4793

Published in Canada by General Publishing Company, Ltd.

Acknowledgment is made to the following publications, in which many of
these stories first appeared:
The American Voice
Conjunctions
The Malahat Review
Open City
The Pushcart Prize, XVI
The Quarterly
Tikkun

Library of Congress Cataloging-in-Publication Data

Williams, Diane.
Some sexual success stories, plus other stories in which God might
choose to appear / [Diane Williams].—1st ed.
p.   cm.
ISBN 0–8021–1452–0 (alk. paper)
I. Title.
PS3573.I44846S65   1992
813'.54—dc20   91–22253
CIP

Manufactured in the United States of America

Printed on acid-free paper

Designed by Irving Perkins Associates

First Edition 1992

1   3   5   7   9   10   8   6   4   2

Oh, my God!

CONTENTS

viii

ix

Some
Sexual
Success
Stories

Plus Other Stories
in Which God Might
Choose to Appear

THE LIMITS
OF THE
WORLD

My adventures have led me to believe that I possess two powerful powders—genuine powders. The "I command my man" powder is one of my powders. When I put this powder on my body, then I will command my man. He will always be my lover whether he wants to be my lover or not. He will be obedient and satisfied, whether that's what I want him to be or not. Nothing will ever take him away, whether that's what I want or not.

I'm not sure what the purpose is of my other genuine powder.

Now what?

What would you do? Would you go ahead and use either of these powders, if you, as I have done, had gone ahead and paid money for them?

Keep in mind, we are past the age of enlightenment. This is past reason. We are pretty deep into modern history and the decline of religion. This is when Nature itself has been stripped bare of its cozy personality and we all feel homeless in our own natures as well.

To say it another way, I gave away a pure love powder with no conditions on its use, or specifications warranted. (A lusty friend of mine grabbed it out of my hand.)

So now what?

Whosoever reads this, write to me if I am still alive, or please write to my children, or to my children's children, who may yet be even still deeper into the farther reaches of our common history. Give us *your* opinion. Provide please credentials for you yourself, who you are doing the talking.

Are you a superior person? Or, how soon do you think you will be? I can ask because I asked.

MY HIGHEST
MENTAL
ACHIEVEMENT

Baby, I will miss you with your common sense, and with your blindness to psychology. My prediction for you is that you will have a fascinating life and that you will stay eternally young, and that you will never lack for love. I am interested in all aspects of you.

If I could know what happened the last time you had sexual intercourse with me, and what your opinion of it was, what your experience was with it, I would be so interested to hear. Could you tell me how this time this sin was different?

The last time for me, when I saw my own hair there beneath my swollen belly, the sight of my hair offended me. I would rather see how I pinned your legs. I had opened my legs for you, and with my saying "This is

5

better for me," I had twisted around onto my side for your sexy behavior. The big baby which was inside me took a beating. In any event, I do believe that sex, or even love, is not inappropriate for the very, very immature.

It is so much better for me to be the one who loves rather than to be the one who gets loved! It is so much better for me not to be the one who can take it or leave it—as you take it. Just think!—I actually became radical at the Grand Canyon when I looked around us and just kept my mouth shut there. It was the full scope of my achievement that I wanted to take a running start and then leap in. Don't forget, I like a mess!

CLEAN

This begins where so many others have ended, where the man and his wife are going to live the rest of their entire lives in perfect joy, so they arrive at the train station.

Now we're on our way. I'm dooteedooteedoing as if I'm happy. Went to the mail where I go to get it. Touched it. Washed myself. Meticulously washed out my contraceptive device with Cascade or Joy.

I toasted a piece of toast for myself to eat, buttered it, put cheese on it, drank coffee I had made, orange juice I had squeezed, took care of the other people. Put away food. I washed. I washed. I never thought I'd get the semen off my ring. The speed of my thought was a deep offense to me. It should have taken me a lifetime to find out how not to be happy just to ensure perfect success.

THE GOOD
MAN

He called it a triumph that he never controlled her passions. That gadget with propellers, with the pads on the propellers, that he had used to produce ultra-pleasure for Darlene—his dream come true—was swell.

He was consoled by this ultra-pleasure briefly. Soon afterward, he died. He was alone when he died, because his pleasure-loving daughter had gone off to the theater.

As a dead man, prone upon his bed, this gadgeteer would be an inspiration either for Darlene or for his daughter.

One day, when he had been alive, so to speak, he had killed a hornet by slugging it, and then, before he realized what he was doing—seizing for himself an opportunity—he had consumed all of the fresh greens which he had heaped up on his platter, plus the strips of the boiled meat. That should have been the test of his manhood, because he is a darling.

PUSSY

The woman's knowledge gives her vicious pleasure. She could have understood sooner if she had only tried to understand. Now that she understands, she will just not leave the men alone, now that she understands that everything that matters has nothing to do with her expectation of loyalty and devotion from a person she is hoping is nearly perfect. Oh yes, now the woman is full of desire as she climbs the stairs to her room. The stairs glow for her eyes. The woman sees a man heads taller than she is jump out at her and then turn back away. He is subtracting things from himself, because she can see only his trouser leg and his one shoe as he goes into her room.

Upon her entering her room after him, the woman does something significant and full of meaning.

Albeit, the orange orange, the thin, dry, oval slice of gray bread—oh no, there was even something more concealed in some silver foil—the elixir the woman knows emanates from these hors d'oeuvres which are all hers, on her tray, on the table, at the end of her bed—amounts to what the woman is if I say so. She equals anything at all on my say-so. The woman is a little dirty thrill.

This is the haunting story of a young man who married for love and who found himself in the grip of a considerable poonac.

TURNING

We kept on and I did not break into tears. Meanwhile, I am wondering which one of us is the cruelest. I can hear my voice saying all of those things.

A few months later, he reminded me that our misfortunes were almost identical, because, he said, we had become inextricably commingled. When he said what amounted to that, I put my arms around him and I kissed him. However, my suspicion is that he cannot tolerate being confined by a woman.

When daylight came, we made our preparations for the day, by bathing, by dressing, by eating. My own appearance was of concern to me, but there was also my great suspicion about what we had been doing throughout the night. Had we succeeded? Should we have been rejoicing? controlling our anger? openly admitting where the true superiority resides? Or should we have kept on with our spirit of rivalry?

Anyway, I spoke seriously with him about my violent disposition. But just around the corner, I did not know what it was.

No sooner had the summer arrived—it was a day like today—with the sea whipped up by the wind, the sky was filled with action—with tumbling clouds, carrying on how they do, erratic, totally unstable, disorderly, maltreating each other's lifeless bodies, fabricating, evaporating ominously. I trust the unknown. I could never be astonished by such painless deaths apart from one episode, wherein I attempted to twist my fate, and to rear a child, among other things.

THE DOG

She had every reason to think that he had had a good time with her when he licked thoroughly with his strong tongue the private parts of her body. She was in bed when he did this. He was her best friend.

When she awoke the next morning, she smelled the sweet lilac and the roses in her garden—she was aware of the thump of his tail—and felt a breeze spring in through the window screen.

She ate a small piece of fish for her breakfast. She hummed a little tune to herself—and when she opened a drawer, she observed an old crumb from some food in there and she thought, This is unbelievable.

Her husband, Frank, came in for his breakfast. Frank is clever, of course.

She said to Frank, *"Sit!"*

Really, she did not understand at that time why Frank didn't.

THE MAN

It was the best week of his life. I wasn't there for
much of it. He used to try to copulate with my
boyfriends when they'd come to the house and
he'd chase around and chase around. He'd come when I
called his name, and I would go wild screaming his
name until he came running to me faster than I could
ever run, so I'd sink to my knees sometimes to get down
on his level with him, with his excitement, which was
often running rampant. His bed was filthy where he
rested and slept. He ate with gusto, made a great noise,
and drank what he drank with a power to drink I will
not ever forget. He influenced me a lot.

REALLY, REALLY, REALLY

Several times while she was wishing, she had looked out over a large body of water. For heaven's sake, she thought she could at least indulge her desire to see something exceptional a couple of times.

She bought a present for herself which she didn't think was good enough, at a huge personal cost, which was too high.

She's never really, really, really wished enough for anything in her life, or for a person, but she had thought she should indulge herself somewhat, so she sort of did. She kept indulging herself somewhat, until she went broke. Her goodwill toward herself was worthy of a king's or of a what?

The next year, when she visited France with her

cousins Tanya, Luisa, and Margo, she went to the market a couple of times. Tanya chided her for being withdrawn. Luisa tried to cheer her up. Margo was indifferent to her.

When she was put into confinement, her hands and her feet were tied, her nose was clamped, and she was force-fed. Once more, a couple of times, she wished she could be a good person and that she would have the wisdom to make safe and sound decisions. This time this little bit of wishing made it so! *And I mean it!*

THE COURAGE
OF A WOMAN

I am pretty sure that everything in our hearts is wise
and pure and chaste.
    He appreciates me. He admires me. Maybe he
even worships me. Well, I worship him and everything
he stands for, such as beauty, valor, intelligence, dili-
gence, gracefulness, loyalty—I don't know if he cracks
jokes, but there *is* such a thing as perfection!

We are very ambitious. We achieve everything a family should achieve—as much as we know about the
goals of a family, what the goals ought to be. We cannot
take ourselves too seriously.

After learning absolutely everything, we could not
make mistakes. We could not make fools of ourselves. I
have heard that that is dangerous.

I stay there most nights in our bed, in our bedroom. I

do not get up off the bed once I get down into it. I am still talking with excitement about this fact, and marveling, how I find myself at the end of an hour still tireless and still safe. We have treasures and luxury. I have just bought for myself a pair of the most compelling earrings with little diamonds. People look at your ears before they look at your hands to see your rings. People may never look at your rings. Marilyn told me that. Marilyn hobnobs with duchesses and dukes and lords and all the nobility. Her life is just . . . it is very similar to mine if I knew more about her.

Marilyn's increasing popularity and reputation have given her personal stature, which I crave. However, in the spring of this year, there has been a distinct turning point in my life. We have just finished building our Sea Forest home and now we are not spending our money as usual. I keep myself hungry, so that I will shed some weight, so that when I look at myself, I am thinking to myself, I could just go ahead and fly.

I was walking humbly down the stone steps toward the sea with my husband, Frank, and with my son Ephraim. Ephraim was weeping.

"What is it?" Frank asked his son.

We had just, I had thought, all of us, been feeling nearly blissful, sitting together on our garden terrace.

I had thought Ephraim was blooming.

When Ephraim spoke, we watched him closely.

"What's the trouble?" Frank said.

For all intents and purposes, my mind is not keen.

THE CIRCUMCISION

The infant is too young to hear the credo he should live by: *He should marry and do good deeds.*

I want to know what is going to happen— you know—will he end up being one of those people? I am one of those people—leading my life. Almost daily, my life is ideal for a person gifted with power and reason.

That the infant was substantially drugged was a good deed. I left without paying any respect, or without saying anything to the infant, because *who is it?*

Walking to my car, I see the other cars available to other people. I put my key into the lock of my car, but my key doesn't fit the lock. I am going to have to stick my key into another one. This is being repeated and repeated and repeated all over the world with impatience or maturity or dead to the world. The ease with which my key finally does do the trick puts a knot in my throat. I am a sad woman. My face is hard. My car is enormous. The road is an outrage that I follow with a blood lust to get to my home to my husband.

Whom I uncritically love.

ALL NEW

When I was still a girl, I did this. When I get to you, you have such a stake in warmth and affection and you are drinking up your wine from a golden goblet. You have out the cracked mixing bowl and your steel spoon for you to mix with. The fire is the blue ring of light on your stove and your music is here. Flutes, I think, and entreaties from a gang of women. I suppose I am supposed to live or die without such a brilliant man as you.

First, I have to climb a hill—not a lucky omen. Then it is easy going until the storm bursts out. In the storm, I hear the shouting. The people swearing to God. Wet again! I am heading to somewhere else I cannot stay, having such a good time, not lost, and I like to take breaths. I have been doing this. I did not make this up.

GOOD LUCK!

A dele Papini is usually no trouble. She is a disciplined, thoughtful, and sensitive person. She is shy and is not often forthcoming about her feelings. In addition, she is nowhere yet near being an adult emotionally. We hope she can have a husband who can establish a trusting relationship with her so that she can confide in him.

On the other hand, Mrs. von Blerke is brazen. She has no trouble saying "Give me pleasure this way." She can even use the word *cli—cli—cli—*

Von Blerke illuminates conflicts. She turns on the lights. She turns up the heat. She calls herself darling. She likes to make herself look gorgeous. She likes to feed herself lovely food that she loves to eat. She likes to assess herself. She likes to make a choice between her freedom and not having very much freedom. She never refuses shame because the shame is too great for her to bear. She likes to anticipate the agony of jealousy. She likes to be trapped by love.

During the interval between ending her first marriage and the rest of her life, Adele Papini began to have her doubts. When she arrived at the concert hall, she stood patiently in the line for her tickets. She was sick with vertigo when she found her seat in the upper balcony. She could think only of killing herself, of flinging herself directly down on top of the grand piano, onto center stage. Curses! that was way way way down there. Her son thought he would kill himself too. He was there with her. This is God speaking, that's how we know. Their morbid concern was keen. It was impossible to tell, for Papini to tell how long it would last, her life. Her son was suffering. He said so. Her husband, there also, was smart and thin. Papini was wearing her black crepe skirt. Her son's trousers were too short. Papini listened when the music began. Mrs. von Blerke waved to Papini. Papini was disturbed by von Blerke's attention. She dimly remembered falling headlong here once before onto von Blerke during the intermission.

As luck would have it, von Blerke's physical aching was profound also. She fell first to her death before the pandemonium, because we play favorites. There is supposed to be a reason, God willing, for a killing.

THE REAL
DIANE WILLIAMS
HAS CAPTURED
THE WHOLE
OF FREUD

My son Eric Williams told me how he'd jump over or he'd jump on top of a car that was going to run him down, rather than go under the car. We were riding in our car then. I was the driver when he told me.

My errand was to get my new nightgown to fit—the silky, soft, shiny, creamy, slinky nightgown that did not fit me when I bought it, that has more flowers than I'd care to count all over it. I was taking my gown to the woman tailor whose husband invited Eric to his boy's surprise party by calling me up on the telephone to tell me about the party.

The two times I have been to the tailor it was very bad weather. This was one of those times. Sleet slopped on the windshield. Pointing to the windshield, Eric said, "If there was nothing there—if you stopped suddenly—I could go right through it and I wouldn't get hurt!" He meant if there were no glass. I knew what he meant.

"That's the way to think!" I said, "and there's no reason why no windshield would not work except for bad weather," and then I was thinking about my beginnings.

I undressed for the tailor and for Eric, too, so they could both see me naked. I could not figure out why. It wasn't required.

At the tail end of her decadent sofa, I stopped, so I did not have to go into her dressing room. I took off my clothing, throwing it all down on the sofa, and then put on the shimmering gown.

She had me stand up on a pedestal from where I admired in the mirror the gown shimmering and shining on me, and I admired her nimbly squatting to put pins into my hem, and she kept both of her knees up off of the floor, which surely was a feat!

Even Eric was jolly—we all were smiling when her husband emerged out of nowhere. My clothing was all back on then, so all of us were wearing all of our clothing, *the hell with that!*

When her husband held on to his belt with two hands, she crossed in front of him to go to the cash register with my money, which is when I admired her shoes. I was looking down. When I saw her belt, I was looking up, and when I saw her smiling—I was looking up even higher into the middle region which was my warning signal to stop looking.

I determined that her husband is sly on this basis— I've determined this on this basis more times than I can count about so many sly people—that a person is sly if the person seems to insist upon keeping a smile on his or her face. I would not smile—that's not fear!—if I had to say what he had to say about me in front of his wife!—but maybe it will make her happy.

The clear plastic cover for the gown on the hanger that she gave me was far more brilliant than my gown is. It's scintillating. The clear plastic cover was also longer than the gown and it's lethal for a tiny tot whose desire is to put it over his head and with it smother himself, as we all know.

When I piled the gown onto the backseat of my car, I had no opinion of the gown except that it was practically a weightless gown.

When I was with her husband, and when her husband saw me walking toward him, and when he said, "God, look at yourself in the mirror! Will you go look at yourself!" I refused to go look at my white skinlike covering.

In conclusion, human beings—my worrying about them—it's over, it's over, and it's merrier!

THE FLESH

As a couple, I admit, they had me transfixed. They were so alike in everything, with their skin still intact, side by side, under our dining room table, close enough to each other to reach out to each other if they had not been all encumbered because of what they were in actuality—slices of cucumber. I scooped them up.

What is missing here is what I did then with them.

That's when all our company came in, our friends and our relatives, not all of them all together, but the stream of their entering our house began.

I was hearing myself say *sometimes*, and *I'm afraid I don't know* and *yes, I do hope* and *think of me*. My friend R. exclaimed "Cliff!" plaintively. Then C. said in a somewhat louder voice than R.'s, "No doubt he will come."

29

Plenty has been missing here all along, in addition to most of the people's names in their entirety, more of what they were saying, also the overtones and the undertones of their major statements.

Later, when everybody had said their good-byes, I told C. that it had all been like a dream—dinner and so on.

He said, "Tomorrow is another day."

I didn't mean for what I had said to make such a muffish sound, from where there was nowhere further naturally to bounce.

This happens, though, to what gets eaten up. That's all my fault Betty McDonald is a doornail.

PENIEL

The child who became a very great president of the United States of America scolded Dr. Tiffany: "You got me in the eye!" because some of the novocaine Tiffany withdrew with his syringe needle from a vial shot into the child's eye on account of the doctor's clumsiness, and the doctor knew it.

For these purposes, *a very great president* means a president who understands the meaning of the word *good* and who is capable of leading the country, and therefore the world, at least several giant steps toward *Good*.

After the child was shot, Dr. Tiffany commanded the child, "Don't move, that's all you have to do."

The nurse attending both of them, holding the vial,

was acting as a nurse for one day only. On all other days the nurse was a fireman at the army base.

There had been another nurse attending also, but she had been jubilant to excuse herself: "You know what to get him!" she volleyed at the fireman; then she had taken off, as if she was flying.

When she did so jubilantly, the child was doing a quick, wild writhe after having been shot. He was lying down. Dr. Tiffany was standing big and tall—the tallest one, with a robin's-egg-blue paper mask, masking half his face, tied behind his head, and the abashed fireman was confronting Dr. Tiffany.

So far the clues are: the word *Tiffany*, probably from *theophany*; *robin's-egg-blue*; *fireman*; and *vial*—the same sound as *vile*.

Whoops, before the presentation of clues, more information should have appeared concerning the child— that the child repeated—he scolded the doctor again.

Dr. Tiffany reiterated, "Trust me, trust me. It's safe, I know, in your eye—because we put it in eyedrops. That's how I know."

The fireman was too abashed to speak.

The fireman never in his life told anyone either the particulars of his masturbatory techniques, and they were manifestly soothing inventions. The fireman knew how to feel as if he was with someone he could love when he was all alone. He should have told at least one other person how.

SPANISH

I wish that everything is enough for Mr. Red who is the husband, who has a heavy Spanish accent. He is a scholar. Mrs. Red speaks English with a heavy Spanish accent also, and she is a full-time scholar, too.

Yesterday, I saw the Reds' bed of scarlet impatiens waving in the wind, which was quite unremarkable. But, that is not all.

Mrs. Red, who is probably responsible for the planting of the flowers, was on her way, carrying her folded-up folding chair and several other things.

She was big enough, even with carrying all of her things, so she could fit comfortably between my thumb and my forefinger from where I sat inside of my house watching her—that was my perspective on my hand.

33

To me, she is like a cutie-pie! like a little doll!

Society, schools, hospitals, factories, and homes are the other victims of the perpetual movement of philosophical thought, as well as many other organees.

A FIELD THAT
CAN NEVER BE
EXHAUSTED

I must let you know how urgent I felt racing down the stairs. We did that—the whole group of us girls. Next winter I am going to be in Florida.

I didn't have any money with me. There was an additional obstacle. Things were probably not that simple. He said, "Follow the good-looking blond!" He was the blond he was referring to, and he was very good-looking, and jaunty, I thought. It was a cute idea to tell us to follow him and to use a line like that. He was having fun I think. Off we trooped. He shouted, "Single file!"

I suppose he had to shout that. I suppose there was no other way to do it.

What do you expect? Don't you expect him to get a little fun out of his job? When he was telling me to pull my pants down, he said, "Pull them down lower."

But how should I tell this? I have been waiting for years to tell this anecdote that any civilization would need to illustrate that there are people, you know, who are perfectly capable of being cheerful.

THEY WERE
NAKED AGAIN

In an instant she may not see it as it happens, how light crowds in and around her red hair, and all around her head, before vanishing into some other light, which is likely having nothing more to do with her hair?—but this is wrong, because there is no inkling of science.

So—I'll get her into his bed, looking at his carpet, which is on his floor, rolled up. Together, they look at it, not for any reason they guess might augment them.

He is prepared to get rid of the carpet. It has been causing him to feel bereft of something he probably never had—something which I could give him.

I could.

She says, "Please don't get rid of it. It comforts me."

I would never say that to him. I would never say that

37

to him in this situation, which is a situation which is a spectacular opportunity for them both, and it is my time they are taking.

You know what happens when they both are thinking so much about the carpet at the same time?

His experience appears to be one of elation, such as finishing. Then she says something obscene, which happens to be clairvoyant. Then I say, "I gave my own carpet away like that, *bitch!*"

But they cannot hear me.

I'll threaten suicide!

You—you think about a carpet.

Me.

THE MEANING
OF LIFE

One point must be made and this concerns what we learn from the history of the world. It must be noted that usually men do not possess valuables or huge sums of money. Their sense of their being sorry about this grows and it grows and it grows. A woman may be their only irreplaceable object. That's why I think the meaning of life is so wonderful. It has helped millions of men and women to achieve vastly rich and productive lives.

Recently, this woman appeared on TV. She has a small head, a big head of hair, and she sings solo. She's wonderful, but because of her dread fear of almost all men, she does not want any more than one man at a time in her life, which is reasonable, but she is always at a loss.

THE BIG
PARADE

The only beginning to this I can bear is "You weren't wearing any!" which a woman who would not hush herself in a restaurant declared. I am asserting she wanted to set another woman there straight, who, with some shame, I suppose, did not hesitate to put her hands up over her ears and to ask anyone at all, "Where are they?"

All of the above stirs me.

All of the above stirs me no more than does the most urgent matter in my own life. The damage is done.

With some difficulty, I could tell you more. I could name *you*, the unnamed you.

Here I am with what has happened. I am not now going to back up and go around to where this is supposed to end by rule, to where I would have to publicly proclaim my loss, as my husband did yesterday, hunched over, carrying my suitcases, headed with his head down—that attitude. I followed him down the big avenue, through the big parade—we cut right through it, and I followed, and there at the big hotel my husband said, "I want to take these inside for you!" and I followed him to where he delivered me personally, so passionately, to my next husband forthcoming.

I had a strangely tender attitude only toward myself then, not toward either one of them, which I have been told is the motive force behind anyone's pursuit of novelty.

THE HAG WAS
TRANSFORMED
BY LOVE

The guys, oh, how you longed for them, round and savory, and just how they get after a few days in their gravy, in the pot, in the refrigerator, and then they are heated up, and then they are eaten up.

I know what Terri Great thought because I remember my thoughts to a tee exactly about my own little new potatoes I just ate, and I am calling myself for the hell of it, *Terri!*

She was sticking her fork—Mrs. Alexander Great—into the little new potato, thinking, I may be the only one who likes this!

For the hell of it, Mrs. Great, you should have stayed there sticking in your fork, tasting and enjoying, and eating up little new potatoes until you had finished all four of your potatoes, *Terri!*

Say it, Terri, from the two and a half little guys that you did eat, you got all the stimulation from the spree you thought was wise, because, if she's going to say, "This is the best it gets from a potato," then Terri Great has stretched her mind beyond the wisecrack fully—stop!

Terri left the house then, and her husband Alexander never saw her again, nor her little guy Raymond, nor her little guy, Guy.

She spent most of her time in the company of people like herself who said they knew what they were thinking. For instance, *she* thinks any penis is ugly.

The enormity of what she had done, leaving her family abruptly, suddenly, and with no warning, gave her lots of other thoughts, too.

She did not upon arrival, speak well the language of the country she had fled to. When she asked a man, for example, on the street, her first day in town, "Where is the train station?" the man told her kindly that there had not been a war in his country for forty years. (He wore a brown, ankle-length, belted trench coat, was about sixty years old.) Miraculously, she thought she could comprehend every word that he had said. It was a miracle, too, that when he flashed it at her, she thought *his* penis was a beauty. Like magic—the colors of it were the colors to her of her own baby's shirt, face, and hat that she had only just left far behind, and the form of it was like a much much much bigger dewdrop.

At home, this rich man had a thin wife. He supposedly worshipped his old wife until old Terri Great came into the picture. Then just forget it. (Things keep happening so perversely for zealots.)

For Terri, she got her first six orgasms during

43

penetration with this man during the next fifteen weeks of their intercourses together.

In the weeks that followed these events, she renewed her days, and she became intrigued with finance.

JEWISHNESS

When the bird was upside down, going along by bumbling, a small one, hanging from the underside of a branch, it was during the snowfall in our mid-April season here. Bobbling? Jerking? An insect would—mice and rats. A bumblebee would do it underneath the branch like that, before returning to its golden world.

The bird then flew up off back the other way, showing me something or nothing I did not understand, like a mood swing.

The experience of getting one to die for me hangs on. I literally ran into it on my lawn, the mouse. It was upside down, with an open mouth, I remember—for cuteness, I bet—a pink tongue behind the teeth.

So I saw the conclusion. I was grateful to see it dead.

I don't have to say how I knew previously about this mouse. I knew where the mouse had been. I had introduced myself into the picture with this mouse. I don't have to say what I was doing to the mouse. I deeply dread it was something wrong. I've told the story other times. Some of my stories get told more often than they're worth. This one is one. It signifies not much. It signifies a story I remember. I remember how my forebears ran like rats escaping, stubbornly clinging, because they had never gone along with an idea—an investment in the future. It was just a grand idea, such as *Hope springs eternal*—but they must have got bored.

THE MISTAKE

S tupid of me, but I am terrified. She is looking at me curiously. The natural thing is to act sympathetic to her, so I go ahead and do that.

Meanwhile, down the hall, a girl is getting angry. I can hear the telltale sounds. This girl comes in to say something.

Stupid of me, but I am terrified. The natural thing is to act sympathetic to her. She is looking at me curiously.

I don't know which horrible thing happens next in my real bedroom. The new carpeting is familiar. I know the bedspread. I know the room well, but I don't remember a clock around here that chimes. I remember mystery, suspense, and adventure.

Even as I blot it out, I was dead wrong to summarize.

47

CLUNK

Stephen still has had no contact with Miss Klinka's hairy pink crack, and we are—even my brother is—spending a lot of time pacifying the aggrieved Mr. Maurer. Meanwhile, Klinka moves ever so slowly, but surely, because I believe in her, toward an evanescent moment that will be worth everything *anyone* has suffered, in my opinion.

I had the opportunity to feel an engulfing anguish that nothing sexual was going on, or would ever go on, between any of these people, because their business happens to be my business, and my business is what I usually think about when I try to summarize my life so far, which has been completely bereft of sex, except for self-abuse.

I self-abuse.

I dropped Klinka off today for her clinic. She needed to bring a sack lunch because the clinic runs from nine to four o'clock. I saw her standing in the doorway of the hut. People were going in and coming out, and a few of her friends smiled at Klinka when she said hello. It's just as I thought—people of all kinds convening, to be organized by the organizers, by the persons in charge of the clinic. All of their arms and their legs were in motion, often—their heads turn and nod—there is some mobility in their faces, some nobility. I wonder why.

I always wonder why.

CHARACTERIZE

The hostess created them in their image.

The cookies are turkeys inscribed with edible names on the butter plates.

There are two cooked, twelve-pound turkeys, no longer in those images, on platters for the entrée, waiting.

The guests are waiting for the entrée, discussing the weather, because winter has not arrived, and one month previous to this time, it should have. (This time, in this place, the winter never does arrive.)

The comments of a husband and a wife about how they feel about the weather prove dramatically to any omniscient thinker that they are dramatically unsuitable, maritally, for one another.

Their infant, who can understand their language better than his own, is listening.

A catastrophic earthquake occurs on another continent in a geographical zone that has never harbored a vicious winter. This is in the country Turkey. There they have certainly had a number of earthquakes in the regions where the winter is mild and only rainy and in those other regions as well.

That's how the cookie crumbles.

No, seriously, my darling, "thou art my bone and my flesh."

ICKY

Her curtains actually do stiffen and then billow into a deformity because of the warm gusts of wind which are periodic. The carnations in her vase tremble when it's their turn, which is poetic. In her beautiful room she is a bit ghoulish even when she is still.

She is also youngish and balding.

She is so lucky because a picture painted by her son in her beautiful room is revolutionary in its scope, scale, and ambition. All of the knowledge her son will ever need to know about ghoulishness is in it.

The son is correct if he chooses to believe that his mother is a ghoul.

He thinks her armchair is as comforting as nobody he has ever known. There are flowers he cannot identify, printed on the upholstery, but their type, he is well aware, is icky. In her beautiful room where he has gotten her riding crop wet, among other things, his mother has stuck his tiny last lost tooth, with glue, onto the frame of her mirror.

A sensational evening is ahead for the boy, even though he is not allowed to bring food or drink into any room outside of the kitchen.

His mother has just asked him to do a couple of odd jobs for money.

ORE

A generally reliable woman was pestering the seed—or is it called a pit?—that she had noticed was blotchy. The reliable woman at work in her kitchen observed privately to herself, for no reason she knew of, that the pit had been discolored by avocado-colored markings. The woman was using her fingers to wrench the pit out from the center of the ripe fruit. The pit was not coming along willingly.

No, this is not about childbirth.

The surprise is that anyone as reliable as she is had not had plenty of experience wrenching pits.

The pear's pit—this is an avocado pear pit—was not of a like mind to hers—like, *What is the matter with you, pit?*

What is the matter with her very reliable husband,

who could not extract this woman, his wife, from their home?

The wife had been making her husband miserable for years, being the unbudgeable type.

I'd say time for a change.

In their secret life, the husband and the wife then sought the usual marital excavations—their aim being to meet their troubles with equanimity.

For starters, they agreed. They agreed how excellent their sexual satisfactions together were, how much more reliably attainable these satisfactions were, more now than had ever been the case before, now that every other aspect of their life together, they admitted, was so unsatisfactory in such extreme.

No, no, no, no, no!

This discussion never occurred. The husband and the wife no longer had the means to conduct such a high-level discussion.

These people are annoying. You know how annoying? To me, as annoying as it was to see for myself last night at twilight one bright sparkling spot in the sky that did not move. It did not get bigger, or brighter, or smaller, or dimmer, and for all intents and purposes, it is stuck there.

As I am.

THE CARE
OF MYSELF

So why can't everything be perfect? God love him, he appealed to me. He had startled me into feeling an incredible amount of affection for a stranger—him. Still, I could have made mad passionate love to him, this inspector who rang my doorbell, who had dressed himself as a fireman.

"Do you have a wound? Is that a bandage on your head?" I asked him.

He tugged on the stretchy cloth which was not supposed to be hidden under his helmet. He said, "We all wear that."

The days and the years pass so swiftly.

Now, what I am doing for my wound is this: I stick any old rag or balled-up old sock I can find as close to it as I can get. Belly-down on the floor, with my reading glasses on, I've also got some filler sticking almost into my asshole. With my bawdy book here to comfort me right in front of my nose—we are both, the book and I, products of a great civilization—I take the plunge. I am thrusting mightily, and sometimes I manage to get hurt again.

CRUSH

There was no Weinberg. The server barging into all that with his tray of only a few nuggets on a doily was peevish with his back arched, with his chin up. A deadly serious woman was introducing Mrs. Williams and a Darnell Hyde. The woman showed me where her waist was and her curved legs were visible to me when she marched over to a dressed-up man to say his name.

The rest of this story is about my family's poignant meal in the elegant hotel dining room. Within striking distance, there is a celebrity who thinks she should be eating here. She is exquisite and brainy and delicately made, it appears—or she is fashioned to appear to be delicate. Her lacy necklace sparkles around her neck. Her lacy bracelet on her wrist sparkles. At her throat

58

her skin is deadish white and, elsewhere, her hair is white. The rest of this story is about my wish to be her. Her escort should be ashamed of himself. His back was turned to me the whole time.

My mother loved the food. I loved mine. I was marginally disappointed in it. I escaped when I said I had to go to the bathroom, the same way I forgot with my hand on the handle of the fridge door why I had wanted to look inside. It is a great natural law, I think, but of what?

Diane, I was the first of us to swoon, entering the glass elevator, descending—my only purpose being to resemble a human being going down.

A PROGRESS
IN SPIRITUALITY

We were in our own backyard, with everything that that could mean, portending. This could be important.

To taste his drink, to look into his eyes, to be shocked, to give my opinion, I had been up on my feet.

"I am shocked. It is so sweet," I said. I was.

He said, "It is."

I sat back down.

The wind took his paper cup, almost blew it away. He got it back. He put it down. He picked it up. No-handed, he bit the rim.

"It's no trouble," I said. "I'll take it inside and throw it away."

My guess is, it was my "trouble" or my "no" he

60

heard, when he saw my shapely form as I turned with his paper cup.

Things got all knocked back—I don't have a clue how.

To have seen his face then—what's it called?—turgid with lust for me?—was a forgotten truth, and tonight I am destined to shoot the rival woman who tried to snatch him. I shoot her by shaking her hand.

When I take her hot hand in mine, we could be the rivals dipped in stone, in the antique story. There should be a story. I don't know the story. There may be a story of them getting a grip on each other forever.

What does that mean? Nobody gets killed. I'm stuck with her. He's stuck with me. All I remember is our kinship, which makes me sick. I have gone so very far to deny death.

It is already only a memory.

THE BAND-AID
AND THE PIECE
OF GUM

There was the possibility up until five o'clock—then there was no more possibility. I expected to hear from Walter today. When I woke up, I was cheered by the thought that maybe today, *today* would be the most important day of my life. Today I ended up using the Band-Aid Walter had given me on my toe. He had thrust it into my hand. "Take it. You never know when you may need it." The piece of gum he had once given me I chewed today finally also. "Try it. You could learn something," is what he had said. Remember how I told you he grabbed me around the neck the last time I saw him? It was practically impossible to walk, which he was trying to do all at the same time, and trying to get me to walk along with him, too.

There was the possibility, perhaps, that we could both have toppled over onto his floor.

That's it. Usually they start where a person was born, then their parents, their parents' parents, where they were born, occupations, so that includes dates, names, locations, character traits of all the parties concerned, chronology, trauma, wishes, dreams, eccentricities, real speech, achievements, including struggle, the obstacles, someone's dementia, another chronic illness, a centrifugal drama, certainly all the deaths, photos, paintings if any—likenesses of many of the parties concerned, plus summary statements made periodically throughout to sum up the situation at any given time.

THIS ONE'S
ABOUT (_____)

T his is being written to explain my sister's most fundamental, the most important discovery ever made in human history so far by an individual. Her discovery—it is so shocking—stemmed from, as in every other sphere of life—a rude awakening.

My sister, who made the discovery, was doing the driving. My mother was in the backseat with the attorney. I was in the front seat next to my sister—the discoverer!

We had the attorney in the backseat scrunched up. This is now thirteen years later, after our fierce journey that night—it was indeed at night.

My sister at the wheel—I forgot to mention she had a lame right arm and bad vision, which had been allowed

64

to go uncorrected, and that, also, she had forgotten to turn the car headlights on. I forgot to say that it is easy to see how this resolved, but all quite obviously was not quite lost.

At the great speed I turned around whenever I wanted to take a look at the attorney when he made his statements. I did not get a look at my mother. In fact, did she ever speak?

At the great speed what did my sister say about everything that hung in the balance—that is—how we were doing, when the attorney told her to check her speed?

Strange as it sounds, I still do not know how clear the danger was then. Speaking for myself, I felt then, This is an important drama. If I were the driver, I would be questioning what our alternatives were for where exactly we were heading.

When she got out of the car, all that was real to my sister was the answers to the questions. At the beginning of life we are not in perfect harmony with the universe. I am fond of my sister's idea, which is slowly gaining favor, that at the beginning of our life, when observers are observing any one of us, metaphorically speaking, they get sick. Most of the observers refuse to observe that all this all really has to do with is *clothes*!

And finally, a big thank you to Chuck Cohen in Highland Park, Illinois, because he gave my sister her idea!

TORAH

I carry this plate of triumph into the school building with my Saran Wrap all aflutter all over my iced cakes. I have iced my cakes because I think everyone nowadays has an expectation of icing on it from a cupcake, as I am sure I do, too.

The corn candies I pushed into the icing are the tough lumps, my vicious triples, my quadruples, the repetition of an idea an idea an idea an idea an idea. Are you keeping track of this as I did? This situation could be handled.

I took control of the situation when the official in the office did nothing when she saw me create a situation in her office. But I gave up control when this official declared that no man had ever hooked his fingers into her vagina and then keenly observed her face, or

66

pleaded to go down on her, or pushed her against a wall into her own shadow and said, "We call this dry humping when we do it in school!"

As it turned out, for no good reason, I tested the woman sorely.

I was wicked.

Yet perfectly delightful when I was God.

AN IMPERISHABLE
ROMANCE

I've been trying to get hold of someone to have some fun with. They both have. Let's pretend nothing is awkward. Three of us abreast, with the ancient and august chapel behind us, and in front of us the alarm was not so great. It was the moon. When he squealed about the moon, what I said was, "You should have seen it this afternoon! It was so big and red!"

I had made a mistake.

The crux of her advice about walking in the cold toward our car, way down the road, was, "You just have to do it." We were not dressed for the cold. As a group, we had looked at her black suede French oxfords because we had wanted to, and she didn't want to get them ruined in the dark. She watched her step. I watched my boots. Yes, they sank into the grass at least an inch, not out of sight. I had told him which of his shoes to be wearing. When we were alone, I had spoken to him while tapping, "I like this and this and this."

Certain things should not be spoken of in front of children. I agree with that. Children should not do certain things, and I agree with that. Thank God, she ran like hell, once out of the car, at her house.

It's a Japanese lantern hanging up there—wildly picturesque—before you get to her front door. Has this person never heard of a *bood*?—my favorite word for it.

NUDE

The parrot's owner gives me information about the parrot that the parrot is molting, or something that is awful—that it hates women. The parrot's owner is also a treasure house of information about libidinous debauches.

The parrot's owner should be a handsome man. He has wrapped himself in a white bath towel. His hair is wet.

His little girl is sort of chirping *She hates me! I just hate her!* about their parrot, as a little girl will. She sort of bounces brightly in her swimsuit with its dots of purplish blue and reddish purple, and purplish pink.

I am wearing my brand-new nude—what the shop owner called the nude. The slip has a crease running down its center, not between my legs, from its having been all folded up inside of a drawer in the shop before I took it to try on.

I bought a robe, too, from that shop, which I could have had in any one of three different colors—which I will not name—the colors. But I could have.

However, when the shop owner spoke to me of underclothes the color of pink ice, I sort of lost hope that I would ever get them, but I have imagined nothing strong or deep or vivid or very dark or bluish in all the pricks I will have.

How could I?

How could I?

How could I?

JEWELING

In the deep dark recesses of her curse, there lay everything she had.

She was an expert diver, but this had nothing to do with that. She opened her purse and she told her friend, "Look in here."

He said, "What?" but he looked inside. He was used to acceding to certain commands.

She was showing him what he had given to her, where she had put his gift—how the thing was situated in the deep dark recesses of her purse.

Someone thought the object he had given her was an object beautiful to look at.

He had just given it to her, and that is where it had ended up being—for the time being.

He needed no special perspicacity to know that she meant, *See how it looks in here, your thing in mine.*

He is a friend in a clandestine, passionate arrangement.

He is mine.

It is my purse.

Now his gift is all mine, with its deep capacity for spectral light. It is as cold and as hard an object as is the love I receive from two men. It is so hard.

I believe in coincidence and providence.

I believe in these two men as I believe in my right hand and in my left hand equally, and in my two eyes, that they are equally mine, and in my ears, and in the two of everything for and on me.

Two created me thereof, in the beginning. Is it precious? It took two to make me what I am.

NAAA

There's the baby who gets the bee sting. In my opinion, there's the baby carrying around a paperweight that, if he had dropped it on his bare foot, would or could have broken his foot.

The mother of the babies has sprained her ankle, and chipped a bone in it, and she is using a cane to help her get around.

Here's where the plot is thickening. Here's the plot: When the baby was stung, at first no one was sure what had happened, but then the mother said, "His arm is getting all pink." Not to go on and on—the sting was discovered on the tip of the baby's thumb. Finally—I was there—at the moment of the discovery, when just then: the baby stopped his crying.

I was the person who took the paperweight away

from the baby. He walks. He's old enough to walk, just old enough, which is why I call him a baby. He was disappointed, but did not appear outraged, when I took the paperweight away from him. "You should not be carrying this around," I said.

If this were an issue larger than the worry about human extinction, I could allow myself to think about it.

Secretly, I believe the paperweight is an item which should never have existed, *ever.*

The facts of the matter are complex, but this baby's power is nowhere limited.

This baby's power is his renunciation of all power.

THE FULLNESS
OF LIFE
IS FROM
SOMETHING

Exploring the front of her blouse herself—she leaned her head down—her nose, her mouth, her eyes became unpleasantly close to the rest of her. She did not feel, however, disgust. Happily, she was imagining a dark rose-red rose on its black bed.

In her present mood, unfolding before her, she saw valleys and shadows upon herself with something else—we'll get back to that—introduced that she did not crave, that had nothing to do with the turmoil of her spirit, nor with her modest capacity as a person.

This was happening not purely by chance. What had happened was that she had said, "The roses are so beautiful."

"Do you want them?" he had said. "You paid for them."

Next thing, he was wrapping the three roses up for her to take with her. Next thing, she had thought about nipping a bud and wearing a bud. Next thing, she had thought about it again, more nipping—because she had not nipped any bud yet, nor had she put any bud behind her ear, nor fastened with a hairpin a bud into her hair, nor stuck a bud into a buttonhole on the front of her blouse, where a bud would barely make itself famous, because it was not a bud that would glow in the dark.

Next thing, when her sister was putting her face unpleasantly close to hers, she was uncomforted by the nearness of her sister, or by the apparent growing kindness of her sister, as her sister talked, talked, talked to her, as officially as her sister could manage to about the void.

SEX SOLVES
PROBLEMS

There is no going back, and no use insisting I have a bath to look forward to. Is four o'clock too late? Dinner, sure.

As I carried the baby off for her bath, I felt I was doing the right thing. It was what I had been asked to do, and I was trying to be helpful. The baby was naked as a baby, and she took up almost all of the sink, and she was slippery when wet, and not at all easy to hold on to, and I don't think I got much of the soap on her, and she kept shutting her head up into the faucet.

"I have an idea," I said. "You better go to bed."

It was the greatest stroke of luck. It was like putting the baby away. I am not a fusser. It was like having any old thing for dinner and not giving a hoot. This is so basic.

The first person who decided a problem could be solved came up with the idea the same way I did.

We are easy lays, too.

SERAPHIM

I suppose that I do have places, a few places, left to wear my mustache to. I have worn it almost everywhere. Before we go, I put on my fur coat inside of my house simultaneous with my putting it on. My mustache is faint and spiky. My coat is thick and dark.

Going around town tends to be sad, like walking around behind a dog who won't go. You wear what you wear. Tonight we are going to the Fontana for pizza. There will be a TV on in there. There will be plastic chandeliers to simulate glass chandeliers. There will be simulated oil paintings on the wall to simulate the idea of things: a woman with a hat on, perhaps her skirt roughed up by the wind, her hand lifted to keep her bonnet on her head.

When the pizza comes, I put a fingertip into my plate to get a crumb stuck to it, then to lick the crumb off.

This is my gift to my children—whereas theirs to me is not to be nasty about having a mother with facial hair.

I am telling you, I never wear it anywhere near my perianal or my vaginal-lips locations. If it as much as touches my eyes, I wash them out with a solution. I promise you—*you are an angel!*—I keep it out of the reach of the children!

NO, CUP

Get the family out forever, out from around the table.

Now, at breakfast, the most important objects on the table are the way-out-of-whack coffee cups for the parents, twice normal size, and their double-sized saucers, all shiny black.

The cups are almost as tall as the normal-sized white pitcher of milk that was there for the children, when the children were there.

The white paper napkin, not nearly as important as the cups are, partially hidden under the biscuits in the basket, and getting soiled by biscuit grease, is sticking up. The points at the corners of the napkin are what stick up the highest, but the points do not reach as high as the white milk pitcher reaches with its lips—*pardon*,

lip. Even so, allow for the possibility that both the lip of
the pitcher and the napkin points express human aspi-
ration, conceptually.

Already, there is too much to think about on the
table. What is the most important thing? One of the
cups should be enough to think about.

Cup.

The shine on the cup.

Light.

No, *cup*.

The most important thing in any circumstance is
what people want to believe is all wrong, you asshole.

Defecation.

MY RADIANT
GIRL

I am not so sure there is a reason to tell this except
for my wanting to say things about magic, about
myth, about legend that might brighten up your
day, if you believe in magic, myth, legend. It was
Coleridge who said we might brighten up the day this
way. Emerson might have said there are real nymphs
in your city park, if you look. Oh I'm sure Cocteau
and George Eliot had their opinions on nymphs. Let's
say Edith Wharton's daughter had the last word. I'm
adding, though. My nymph in Central Park I did not
know was a nymph right off. I believe thoroughly in
her now.

The nymphs don't have to be little. She was. She had
removed most of her clothing. Men watched. There she
was, oiling herself—an unblemished beauty with her

teacup breasts, with boy hips, covered by her sunning suit, which she had had concealed under the other clothes, a necklace rimming her neck, and yellow hair tied back.

She looked at nothing except to do the sunning—to take care of the oil, her skin, and how she should rise up, or she should lie down, or turn—she had to look. Two men next to me, whom I also earnestly watched, watched earnestly.

I'm a woman. You don't take that for granted, I suppose, or that I believe in ghosts just because I say, "See the nymph!"

As Yeats said, "There are no such things as ghosts. Ghosts, no! There are those mortals who are beautifully masquerading, and those of them who are carried off." Okay, as Yeats did not say.

Sometimes girls like her are gotten rid of in a not so gentle way. Socrates said of one, "A northern gust carried her over the neighboring rocks, because I said so." He said, "I was swollen with passion." Nietzsche said the people of the cities have the machine to get rid of them if they are annoying.

It was Captain Stewart who informed me that because I saw the girl, "You will rise to the summit of your power, then you will die a violent death." He said that. His records confirm this fact.

So far, I have told the truth. It was straight from my heart to say we would be killed.

HE AWOKE
AFTER A
LONG DREAM

The long-lost friend appears and I can barely recognize her. But, of course, she must be who she is, even though she looks to me entirely different in all aspects. We go to an old familiar place I had stopped going to, but had started going to again. I had said I would never go to that place again ever. I had stopped going to that place entirely.

It's what I love about my life—my guess that my silence, my absence from her had given her pleasure, had given her some peace.

I am old-fashioned. What I should have done is died.

We pay the taxi driver and continue in the direction of our happiness. Her hand is holding my hand. I say, "Are you going to stay here with me forever or not?"

"I don't know," she answers gravely, "but I bet that you can guess."

Then there is this splendid silence.

We can do it together, I see, what we can do together apart.

CANNIBAL, THE NATURAL HISTORY

E verything was so bad because of what happened in the spring, but I eat it.

I asked Chuck, "What happened in the spring?"

Something very very bad. I couldn't get to what without Chuck's help. The reason to remember was to keep talking to Chuck for X amount of time.

Chuck said, then I nearly said, the *drought*. He said it first.

"Is there good news?" I asked Chuck.

I did not address Chuck as Chuck, who was unaware I knew his name or his secret.

Chuck answered me spitefully. "They are ripening them artificially."

Spiteful Chuck. I knew. The secret about Chuck was

that everything was nice about Chuck except that he did not know how—*anything* about being nice. Something else about eating—the train of my thought—in X amount of time, nowhere near Chuck, I got to it—it was mothers who would not knowingly eat a coward before their babies were born. Among these people, the diet restrictions were severe. Strict for a purpose.

I'm a mom like that. Not to brag, today at lunch, Maggie did not smell it on me, what I have been cooking. She guessed wrong. *Chuuuuuuck!*

I know one thing about Maggie. She is a very, very mixed-up person.

BLOOM

The ham, the sweet and the tender cookies, pecans—heavily grooved the way they are—candies wrapped in green foil, in red, or in any foil, are the custom, so is the attitude of the little girl named Sandy.

A man and a woman, not married to each other, who had just returned, they said, from a romantic holiday together in Capri, took turns to speak to each other respectfully of their spouses and I listened in. One attractive man was there. Well, I like him.

I leaped to my feet to go over to the attractive man, and Sandy followed me. Since then, many others have tried to stick to me like glue.

Please believe me that there is no part of me which is sad, angry, or resentful when I remember suddenly leaping up that time, or many other times since this time or before. The cause of my serenity may be that I am not ashamed to just go through the motions of having naked power and ambition, as in fucking.

This burgeoning is gratifying.

MEAT

The prince's house makes me feel respect for his house. The house causes me to stand and look at his house as if his house deserves all of my attention. I will need to be butted out of this drifting off into full respect for his house by something necessary or urgent, and nobody will get me to speak about my mother's new boyfriend instead of the prince who lives in this house.

The first time I met the prince, he was talking to his hired man inside of my neighbor's garage, and he told me to come by sometime and we could have an Ovaltine at his house.

I just don't want to say why we were all in the garage. It is not even as germane as the rumpled prince on the edge of his property today, talking with the three hired men. His hair, his shirt, his trousers were rumpled.

There was a rather smooth aspect to the shirt of one of the hired men, how it stretched itself smoothly down, then down in under and behind his belt, which reminds me of the food galore at my mother's boy-friend's party, which an overweight woman dressed in white with bleached yellow hair prepared and served to us—meat.

I loved Gwen—the woman sitting next to me at the party. She bakes her bread in a machine. It doesn't swirl, but since it is better to be impetuous, she puts into it anyway cinnamon and raisins into the white dough!

I am tempted to not say anything more which could imply anything, because this is not literature. This is espionage.

N.B. If you like, change all the words.

93

THE STRANGEST
AND MOST
POWERFUL

"Look, we've been over this and over this."

I giggled. I began to blush. I stammered, "You—you—Dicky—I—"

It was all unnecessary because—*blaaruah!*—the doorbell rang. Behind the window adjacent to the door, I saw a face and a fist.

Where we all were, at my aunt and uncle's house, was a particularly lovely spot. A group of people not yet too terribly tired continued making comments while I sat in a trance. My uncle opened the door. I heard my uncle say, "No, I won't do that," then another man's voice, "Why not?" then my uncle, "I am afraid," then the other one, "Poor girl, she's the kind who gets taken advantage of." "What on earth do you mean?" my uncle said.

A certain kind of shock had set in, which protected me. I thought of going home. Of course, I made no attempt to leave. I was puzzled, and as per usual I spoke up. I did not comprehend or enjoy what I said, despite all of my experience talking. Then I laughed, and turned away with embarrassment. The next thing I imagined myself being spoken to. My uncle was handing me a drink, and a big stranger, with a purple orchid in his buttonhole, with his hair combed down flat, stood beside my uncle, gaping at me.

Clinkety-clink! clinked the ice cubes in my drink. I spilled some of my drink, of course, on my sweater, when the apparition began a conversation, which constitutes our culture. It seemed so trivial, our culture.

THE SEDUCTION

You try so hard when they are sick. He's very sick.

When I cooked, I'd cut up a little liver before I left, and he ate it. Do you think that's good?

He is a significant figure. There's a treatise on him I am reading now. There is to be a thoughtful conclusion forthcoming, I hope.

It took a long time for historians to develop the notion of objectivity, because of their compulsiveness, which is a never-you-mind that overcomes logical thinking.

This calls for an explanation. I'd say it does.

Let me see: Do I remember? I ask myself. Let me see: YOU ARE TOO BIG! I did not know what to do. I did not know if I was pushing or if I was just trying to push. I did not know the difference.

Despite the promising start—I was so excited—things went badly, but I haven't spoken ill of him. I've heard others say, "What a bastard!" I've heard his dreadful sobbing. He has clutched at me. He has spoken reasonably.

"Yes," I said.

"Darling," he said, and I got frightened. And then he said, "I was afraid to touch you." I let him hold my hand. I could not tell what he wanted—a theatrical marriage? I'm sympathetic to the most simple human act.

HA

"See if you can find a whistle, even a toy whistle, *any* whistle," she implored.

He knew he'd never find one in their town. When you know how it will turn out, you feel tired. So do I.

There ought to be a brilliant portrayal of the homecoming—the boy with what? or with the lack of what? the matriarch to be reckoned with.

An hour later, the boy returned with nothing to say.

After her hesitation, his mother asked, "So?"

He heard her clanking their plates.

But instead of answering his mother, the boy went back out into the backyard.

Because the mother's confusion was even greater than her boy's, she said nothing more either. But oh, how she thought!

Oh, this is hopeless! she thought.

What would her boy's fate be? she wondered. Well, she decided, they need a victim. I need a victim. We all need a victim.

The boy's heart heaved. He thought he was confident of the future. His house had been through fire. Things needed doing.

As for his mother, her voice had positively no timbre. She barely got her words out. In real life, she was barely heard.

About other details—or more about the boy—I don't have any ambition for any more, except to observe that the boy squatted on his haunches in the flowers.

The mother remembered then—that, as a baby, he had looked a trace displeased to be born.

THE REVISION

Y ou should not read this. It is too private. It is
the most serious. It is even too serious for me. I
should make something of this.

Here is the best part, when he said to me *come here*.
That was the very best part of my life so far. In the
doorway to his bathroom was where I was. It was
where I was when I asked him, "Are you peeing?"

He said, "No, but now I am." He was seated to do
the peeing, so it would not be any problem to do it,
facing me. I didn't even hear it, the peeing, if he peed.

Well, why?—why can't all of it be dirty parts, every
part a dirty part, or quickly leading to another dirty
part?—the part when he just put himself into my
mouth?—or the part when he said *you looked*—I can't

remember how he said I looked to him, with that part of him in my mouth, but he jiggled on my jaw. He said *open up* before he went ahead and he peed.

Oh! That's how babies could be made!

THE EARTH
IS FULL
OF HER GLORY

Mary Lugg had not perceived her fate. It would seem so cold-blooded, wouldn't it? a planned thing. She stood straighter to see if that would help her back feel better. That helped. Then she put herself into her chair at the table.

Alan Hatt was speaking, "—for years. That's what I think. In my opinion, you deserve it."

"It's witchcraft," said Amanda Hatt.

Rod Rowan had a toothache. Rod Rowan whispered, "I can understand it."

Alan Hatt had a brain tumor he knew nothing about. Nobody knew if it would eventually kill him or if he's to die of boredom.

Mary Lugg said, "She's a good cook. Don't tell, but I

can't eat these." Mary Lugg was referring to the dump-
lings in the soup. She could not eat them.

"It was a horrible experience," Rod Rowan said. "I
told them everything."

"Good Lord, Rod!" cried Alan Hatt. He grabbed the
edge of the table for support.

If the truth were audible, the actual world was moan-
ing. It began to dawn on Mary Lugg what was happening. Her thought produced a fine dramatic effect, not
unlike what she endured whenever she lied, or when
she got what she wanted. It felt good.

THE TIME
OF HARMONY,
OR CRUDITÉ

I would say I was half the way through when I thought to myself: Be careful. Anyway, there were twenty of them, to begin with.

I cut every one in half.

There were six.

I cut one to pieces, wedge-shaped. I'd say there were nine wedges. This is the estimate, generally, I get from thinking back on it.

I cut slices from it.

I'd say there were six slices.

I sawed and I sawed back and forth.

I cut stalks. I made chips. There were about fifty more wedges. There were wheels. One wheel which I had produced took off, rolled along, and dropped. I made sticks and I made slivers. I made raggedy bunches, stalks, chunks.

The house was neat and clean as ever. I got a lot of things done. I fully enjoyed sex. It turned out I was very deep into being.

On so many occasions, what goes with what? I do not want to leave behind anything during the accumulation that I will have to grasp at one glance because it is not a piece of crap.

BEYOND
PRINCIPLE

I t predestined her to become a thinker, to become a woman in a storm center for many years to come, because she did no fornicating with any other. She never left him out of it, *never*, not before she met him or after she had met him.

Into her mind she liked to keep adding what she called "a little curve" or "a little fork" among the pathways. She was ready to change her mind. Original conclusions were not her aim. She preferred to lay claim to the obvious.

One time when her hands were on his naked flesh, he said, "I love it when you draw me in." Squeezing his rump, "Like this?" she said.

Doing her job, she thought, *Who says that men aren't soft?* and the one man became the multitude through the backward path that leads to satisfaction, toward the upshot of all far-fetched speculation and curiosity— which is an example for example of how she first thought her idea of giving herself a little pinch or little pushes, of getting her hand up in between her and him in the very middle of their act. Not seeking to interrupt, to fail shamefully, or to baby herself, she intended to be serious—not to goof up, not to fuck up. "You're going to have fun with it, I know," she said. She thought, *I want to know how this turns out*. She said, "Come in and show me." She wagged her finger.

She cut him out of her life.

Isn't she wonderful, if an assumption is permissible? It looks as if she ended those embarrassing situations at any cost.

Her terrible war gave rise to pathology of this kind, but her terrible war finally put an end to temptation. Now I could throw in something that's so sensual, that's full of an object.

SCRATCHING
THE HEAD

W e respect her from learning from her. Let us compile the factors of her failure. We could not find hereditary factors. We said, "Tell us about yourself."

At the zenith of her life, in her mid-forties, she changed. She met the man who awakened her oldest erotic feelings.

"What a nightmare!" she said. "Why can't it be over? When I touched his arm, my hand was on fire. When I am nowhere near him, there's a sledgehammering down here."

She gestured, not shyly, toward her genitalia. She inquired, "I have never heard of that. Have you?"

Perhaps we should leave the question as it is.

She asked herself aloud, "Do I have the moral force to finish my life?"

Her *phleglomania* was the *phenomenomenom* that had set in. Her highest average speed of forty-five miles per hour she achieved in her automobile. Sometimes she briefly closed her eyes, she said, while driving, because, she said, "What could possibly happen?"

She had a regal calmness. That should sound familiar.

Her instincts for victory, her naturally fierce nature, the entire inheritance of her species, the will to seduce and ensnare, all her cruel powers were melted into a cordial, into a very old sweet, smile—but that's what's been said.

Let us endeavor to sum up. How much repetition does it take? A perseveration? Biological investigation is required to explain the impulses and their transformations—the chief traits of a person. It is easy to forget, not that we ever should, that everything in this world is an accident, including the origin of life itself, plus the accumulation of riches. We should show more respect for Nature, not less. An accident isn't necessarily ever over.

IDEA

The sound our feet made when we walked across his floorboards was a rhythmic accompaniment to physical desire both of us could have thought to put a stop to. It did occur to me, just on principle, to end that noise.

When I took off my coat, he said my coat was gray. I said it was green. He said it was gray.

In the upstairs of his house, when I sat myself down to look around, I decided I liked everything I was looking at. There was nothing I did not approve of, or that I did not admire that I could see.

He said, "You make such fast moves," when he was kissing me. Then he said, "The watch—you have to take off the watch." Into the palm of his hand I put my watch, my four hairpins, my necklace made of silver beads.

He said, "That! Put that in your purse. I don't like that!" when I took off my brassiere. It remained there, though, curled up on his wooden floor, curled awkwardly for a piece of clothing, not awkwardly if it had been something else perhaps, a creature.

He said, "Now," he said, "use both of your hands so that I will feel you are really with me." Or, I was the one who said that to him—that's right, because I knew he could do things he would never want me to do. Add to all of that another distinctive feature, an atmosphere of awe, and something else that could be wet and gleaming which would not ordinarily be symbolic.

ORNAMENT
OF BEAUTY

I received some news, gossip really, which had already gone stale, about this person. I remember
the pair of hands of this person. In July, this person
and I confessed our love. This resulted in countless
tragedies. Why this was is none of your business. On
my birthday it was back to ordinary life. I'm having a
big bunch of orchids sent to another person I know out
of state whom I don't feel I should speak to anymore,
even though we are on excellent terms.

I'm sure I already knew that they are the longest-
lasting of all flowers. The florist says, "Orchids!"
which—those are the first special flowers I ever knew
about! I did too know about them. What if I forget?

The florist is a cheerful young woman, wearing nothing decorative, except—I take that back—a multi-

colored belt. Her shirt is an ocher cotton shirt. Her skin is what people must mean when they refer to such skin as alabaster. I intend this as an idle compliment about her skin.

"Six of them!" is what is spoken loudly by another customer in the shop. With apparent interest he inquires what kind of flowers he is buying. The effort of speech seems too great for him. He stands out like a shining light.

IT BECOMES TRUE

Someone said, "See!"

I saw the chimpanzee doing some of its typical twists and it was flourishing its tail par excellence up in a phony tree. We're all here for a party.

If I said I love this, then what would happen to me? "I love this!"

Nowadays it comes to the surface. This is the zoo. I am at a party which will be of considerable benefit to the zoo.

And fortunately for me, I got myself squeezed up in the arms of a man.

A good ways away from the monkey, we were dancing in a tent. There was not one whiff of the monkey. The man swept me off my feet. It was my privilege. He swung me around. For this, I will always, always be grateful to him. I love this! Also, he surreptitiously slipped his hands along my body, lightly, so I would not notice, out there in front of everyone, while we were dancing. I was so grateful. I loved that.

It was not crude to break away to eat our food, to stick our forks into it by the prevailing standard.

There was nothing crude about my breasts popping up, the tops of them, when I just sat—the corresponding evidence pretty much up for grabs.

When did it happen?

I looked in vain for just one member of my family, or the most prominent person in my world. I was so grateful.

Typically, we are left, so many times. I love that routine—the horns of my dilemma—when they try to drag me forcibly away.

GOING WILD

It is a dirty lie that there were no promises at this event in any shape or form because there was food. There was also a discussion concerning the intellect of children. There was a child sucking a green lollipop and being admired by an adult for being adorable while he was sucking, lying down.

Based on my intuition, my dead father would not have had fun at this event.

I had some fun while I stuffed myself to the gills with the food until I was uncomfortable and then I was no longer having fun.

I petted the head of a two-and-a-half-year-old boy and by doing that I modified his behavior. I did not scare him into changing. I succeeded with him by petting him while he was doing something—

anything—and then I was redirecting him gently toward something less appropriate for his age.

We all stopped what we were doing, even I had stopped my chewing, and we had orchestrated ourselves to stare as a group at one child who acted as if he knew he should be center stage. I could have asked myself, What does this child wish for more than anything in the whole world?

Maybe there is one correct answer!

The one person who was giving me the most attention at the event is gone! evaporated right out of my sight! He's off into the pure air of my imagination where I imagine him with me lying down in a bed, where we discuss by what method everything is ordered.

Has there been one grand enough moment of either sex, or serenity, of soothsaying, or of silliness at the tragedy, during which time we paid homage to one object, or to a notion, or to one of us?

Thanks for letting, letting me even address you.

Satisfied is what I am.

CORONATION

A royal person, wearing a royal robe, with something royal on his head—something exciting—there are other smudges, other noble people with him, fine furnishings, and precious objects, and so on. From where I sit on my toilet, the chrome soap holder, built into the wall, is looking great.

This magic makes me wonder. The concaveness is going convexly. It is a grand, miniature, several-storied window to look through, or a glass revolving door.

My *New York Times* I am going through inspires me to think about our Colonel North and about other terrors today which are described.

What is this like? (No answer.) Is this like anything familiar? (No answer.)

Are you familiar with this? (No answer.)

I will answer that it is the burden. It is intellectual work which is as degrading to do as being in the presence of some very great person.

It is so similar to bowing to regard the genitals.

What is it that I would like right now?—to suck a very clean penis? (Yes.)

I am very embarrassed.

INTRIGUES, SCHEMES, AND INVOLVEMENTS

I have seen people do it when they pretend to die. They get up and then they fall down, just as I did. What a little fool! I loved every minute of it. But there was no minute in it. That's a faint, or a slight faint—because it didn't last.

It reminds me of several other times—as on November 9, 1988—when I was sharing with my special somebody a double bedroom, which had a very corny and a very stupid decor. I was pleased with the affection we were also sharing. We called each other sweetheart. We were never cold or unwelcoming. We were happy in our union. The series of shocks occurred then. The situation was explosive. It was clear I was being pushed out, that there was a dark plot against me, that there was outer darkness, that a stylish marriage was inconceivably in its last few days.

My fear of assassination intensified. When November 10 of that same year finally arrived, there we were at dinner. Walter Rogers stated that he was overcome with relief for me. He said he cared nothing for my humiliation. I was no longer worried about what the world would say, for it would be lies, all lies.

But to my horror, the situation seemed to suggest that the remarkable Errol Ferdinand, whom I had hoped would satisfy my needs, was now penniless. Besides, we were both such bad fucks.

Life would now move very, very slowly. There would be unendurable pain in my secret heart, and there would be no break from it until the morning.

HAPPY

The child arrived in the nick of time to eat a pancake. She wasn't trying to escape from sadness, and she wasn't dying for a pancake, but she could handle a pancake standing up, without using a plate or a fork.

The wife wasn't eating yet, but she was cooking and preparing to serve. It meant so much to the wife to do that. Her husband would be served. The wife must have given him an ultimatum. He wore pajamas. The wife wore daytime clothes. The child was dressed for the occasion, and wore these sturdy toddler shoes.

Surely it is a fact of experience, that a young enough child who believes that pancakes are delicious, usually embraces an opportunity to eat one. At the age of two, this child considered her opportunity and made a decision that was plausible to her at the time. However, as an adult who is a happy-go-lucky person for no good reason, she marvels at how jubilant she was, so young, when she missed out on a pancake in a circumstance when nobody preeminent was sneering at her.

THIS IS
THE REASON WHY

He must feel like a complete failure. He is not successful. That's an exaggeration. But it is unclear to him how complete his failure is. Every single one of his—that's an exaggeration, but two varieties of his voluntary aims have been misunderstood by those who would prefer to describe this person as the conscience of humankind. (I think he looks like Ted Forberg.)

One of those keen to know the real facts about him—his own son—feels frustrated. This is the son of his who tried at age ten to set the house on fire with the kitchen matches, the giant wooden kind. The boy could not give himself all the time in the world, yet he did put burn marks in the carpet. He filled a room with smoke and the smell of burnt fiber. He was interrupted before he had the opportunity to be successful. He was a failure. He must have felt like a complete failure. This is an exaggeration. But whenever he feels frustrated, he gives himself all the time in the world to feel frustrated.

Look at how he does his work in a dishevelment, in a chaos, forbidden to be alone with his wife, not entitled to a telephone, not in very good shape. For more than twenty-two years he has put his whole heart into his work, which is tantamount to a souvenir or to a good-luck trinket, his heart is, or to a bangle he has signed, numbered, and inscribed with an expression of his affection for someone. Darn it, if he would only want to do his work.

Anyway, I think I have tinkered with this enough.

THE CASE
OF THE COLD
MURDERER

Getting the lid off the stuff, Mrs. Lewis knew, might mean she would save her son's life, so she worked at it. You uncap it in extremis.

The doctor had advised her by telephone to give it to her son. "This will work if you say to him it will work."

Louella Stack always said it was a simple death, this kind, although unexpected. One feature in the matter was Glenn Gould's playing piano to accompany the death. To get him calmed down—not Glenn Gould—Mr. Lewis embraced his gasping son. The mother, Mrs. Lewis, tried so hard to uncap the bottle.

The prescribed medicine, in these cases, tastes lousy.

Not long before he died, the son—who is also a suspect, actually—shrieked as best he could at Mrs.

Lewis, "You have hurt me so much! I don't want to be your son! I can't breathe!"

Nobody denied any of this.

But perhaps if I speak to him . . .

Regrettably, the parts you will not hear are the parts that sound the best, as I, your host, shrewdly unravel the tangle of motives and human relations. For instance—I'll mow the fucker down—who is this fucking Stack? Was she really worth the mention?

THE LEADER

In just a little while I was not yet so weary that I was furiously working on the secret of life, of my life.

The words in my mouth are uncontrollable the way they come out to speak. Fluently I say: He is a Jew, but who am I?

The Jew laughed, and he said coercively, before he stripped himself naked, before he became the master of my body, before he tickled my slit, before he tugged on my slit, before he tugged it, before he tugged on it, before I was so hard on his hard-on—he said it coercively to me: "Don't be so silly."

"You must let go of me," I said.

Wisely, the Jew said, "This is what it always comes to."

I struggled to my feet. I was profusely kind, too,

before going any further. Then the Jew got up, too. He is by temperament eager.

We were near a patch of trees where there was a family—I think a family excited by fury. Not one of them—the three little girls, a mother, and a father— looked to me, in any way, calm, or happy, or prepared quite yet to be the leader of the family.

Nor was that all: Underfoot, there were heavy tree roots popping up everywhere, and acorns, some crushed, some with, some without their tiny whatnots still on, all of which—this spectacle—was not useless to me, for I can speak for the Jew, too, such is my destiny, that in full daylight our eyes were open not with horror, not to see a fearful end, but to realize—I realize a certain sort of family should probably gather more often as a group to be a witness to love. It was thrilling when the youngest girl asked me, "Did you ever get caught before?"

"Well, sure," I answered her, "and up yours."

MACHINERY

He moves around in his gloom and then he does something with something. He is calmer about his longings.

He sits for a bit before he hears whatever it is. Hearing it gives him the sensation of holding on to a great instrument which is at work.

He discovers a small square white cardboard box and he opens it. Inside is a disappointment.

His children hold him responsible for everything he does. His house suits him.

For some idea of the full range of tools at his disposal, one would have to know what human longings are all about, a calm voice says calmly.

PERFECT

"You want an insight? I'll give you an insight," said a perfect stranger at the children's ball game. Then he gave me his insight, which proved to be exactly correct.

"People will cheer him when he gets himself up," the man said.

I had thought that the child's ankle was probably shattered—that was *my* insight—that the child would not be able to walk, that he would need to be lifted and carried, that he'd never walk again. I thought, Now he is a cripple for the rest of his life.

"He's fine," the man said. "I know he's fine, because, you see, he's hiding his head. He's hiding his face. He's making such a big deal. I know. Sure, it's very painful."

The man had told me that the hardball had hit the child in the ankle. I didn't know where.

I said, "How do you know? It might be shattered. He's not moving."

"Because he missed the ball—" the man said, "because he wants everyone to forget he missed the ball, that's why he's making such a big deal."

If I could have an insight about this man's insight, I could probably save myself. That's my insight. I could save my children, my marriage, the world, if I could let enough people know—that there's a powerful solution in here somewhere—a breakthrough trying to break through.

The stranger was so angry talking to me. I don't think he believed I was believing him, and I didn't.

Will you please rise and Shame us not, O Father.